DESTINY
THE GRAPHIC NOVEL

I0692275

CREATED BY

D.V. NOBLES & MICHAEL GLOVER

DESTINY -THE GRAPHIC NOVEL, EPISODE #2, "THE PILOT" Published by DVNobles Publishing.
Copyright © 2019 By D.V. Nobles - All rights reserved.

Story, concept and design, all artwork, models, layout and final production created by Michael Glover and D.V. Nobles. Destiny and the Destiny universe, including but not limited to, characters, ship designs, set designs, device and technology concepts, story and story concepts are the sole creation and property of the co-creators. This is a work of science-fiction and any similarity to persons living or dead or to other fictional works is purely coincidental. Any reproduction of this work or the use of Destiny concepts or designs in whole or in part are by permission only. The creators of Destiny wish to acknowledge the Blender Foundation (www.blender.org), MakeHuman (www.makehuman.org), Adobe (www.adobe.com), Digital Anarchy (www.digitalanarchy.com), and www.textures.com.

OUR STORY CONTINUES...

In **2259**, during implementation of the **ESC Destiny's** new **Singularity Drive**, something went horribly wrong. A rift in space pulled the ship towards destruction. **Captain Massey** was forced to issue the order he hoped he would never have to give: All crew abandon ship. By sacrificing the ship to the rift, the spatial anomaly began to collapse upon itself, allowing the crew to escape in lifepods. Most of them made it out alive. Some did not.

Destiny was lost.

Upon returning to Earth, instead of being allowed to mount a search for their lost ship, **Captain Massey** and **Commander Jackson** were accused of negligence. **Captain Massey** was ordered to relinquish his command authority within the **Earth Space Consortium (ESC)**. **Commander Jackson's** entire body of work to develop the **Singularity Drive** was confiscated. No search and rescue mission was ever launched. No investigation into why the **Singularity Drive** failed was ever performed.

Having no resources to find the answers on their own, **Commander Jackson** was able to provide one small glimmer of hope for his Captain. He gave him a device capable of receiving the **Destiny's** emergency beacon signal. He cautioned his friend that the signal may never come.

Life went on. **Captain Massey** never gave up hope that one day he would find her...

25 years later, in the wee hours of the night, the receiver began to glow and a shrill sound brought **Massey** abruptly out of a dream. He picked up the device and looked at it, thinking he was still dreaming and, if not, the device must have finally malfunctioned. He contacted his old friend with an urgent message to come as quickly as possible. He needed to know if the signal was real. Because if it was...

Once the signal was verified, the two friends quickly put together a plan to investigate. The signal's origin was from deep space. They would need a ship.

With the help of the **Destiny's** former Pilot, **Captain Kayla North**, the two set out on their quest - a voyage to the stars, not knowing if they would find what was left of their old ship or only a jettisoned black box with an emergency beacon signal beckoning their return.

With their fuel nearly depleted and no way to return home, **Massey** deperately tried to lock on to the elusive signal again and again. Finally, the signal returned a positive identification and lock. The **Destiny's** exact location was confirmed.

When he saw her, dark and desolate, tumbling end over end in the cold, black void, **Massey** was quite sure he still must be dreaming...

Now, aboard the derelict **Destiny** with less than two hours of air left, the two old friends continue to search for the answers to what happened to their ship so long ago...

CAPTAIN CHARLES MASSEY COULD **HEAR** METAL WARPING AND RUBBING TOGETHER FROM THE CENTRIFUGAL FORCE OF THE SHIP ROTATING END OVER END...

THE MOANING AND GROANING OF **TONS** OF STRUCTURAL SUPPORT AND BITS OF DEBRIS HITTING THE HULL.

...AND

THE **DEAFENING SILENCE** OF BEING SO FAR FROM CIVILIZATION IN THE COLD, DARK VASTNESS OF SPACE — THE SILENCE OF A SHIP WITHOUT HER CREW...

EPISODE 2: "THE PILOT"

ON BOARD THE DERELICT **DESTINY**...

HOW'S THE PROGRESS ON THE ENGINEERING DOOR, JAX?

SLOW, CAPTAIN. I MAY HAVE TO GET A LITTLE MORE...FORCEFUL. HOW DO THINGS LOOK ON THE BRIDGE?

SHE APPEARS TO BE JUST AS WE LEFT HER. IT'S STRANGE, THOUGH... BEING HERE AFTER ALL THESE YEARS...

MISS ARROWAY'S OFFICE...

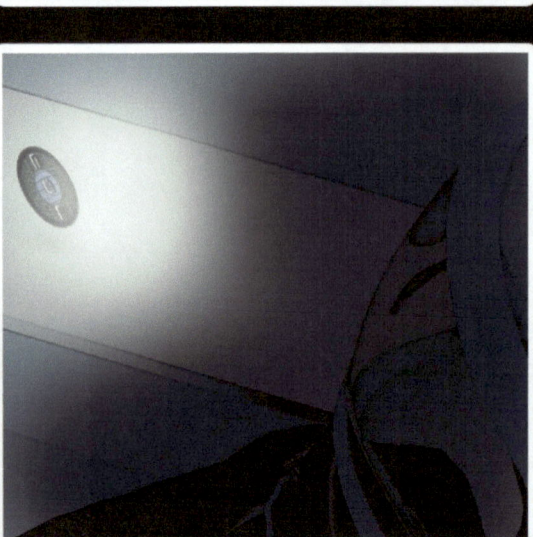

HA HA... KAYLA NORTH'S ESC PATCH. I WONDER WHY AMELIA KEPT THIS...

WELCOME ABOARD THE DES—

YOU! WHAT'S YOUR NAME?

ER...CREWMAN FIRST CLASS JAMESON, MA'AM.

WELL, MR. JAMESON, YOU MAY WANT TO MAKE SURE THE AIRLOCK COMM IS OFF BEFORE YOU RUN YOUR MOUTH! YOU'RE FIRED! GET IN THAT SHUTTLE NOW, YOU'RE GOING BACK TO EARTH. YOUR BELONGINGS WILL BE SHIPPED TO YOU LATER.

BUT, MA'AM I DIDN'T MEAN —

AND YOU...DO YOU WANT TO JOIN YOUR FRIEND OR ARE YOU GOING TO ESCORT US TO SEE THE CAPTAIN?

CAPTAIN MASSEY'S OFFICE

I DON'T CARE WHO YOU ARE, MISS ARROWAY, YOU DON'T DISMISS ONE OF MY CREW WITHOUT DISCUSSING IT WITH ME!

CAPTAIN, YOU NEED TO HAVE A CLEAR UNDERSTANDING OF WHY I AM HERE. THE ESC IS NOT HAPPY WITH HOW THIS SHIP IS BEING RUN! YOUR PRIMARY GOAL IS TO OBTAIN NEW RESOURCE OPPORTUNITIES FOR THE ESC. INSTEAD, WE GET REPORTS OF YOU INVESTIGATING THINGS LIKE QUASAR PHENOMENA AND EXOPLANETS.

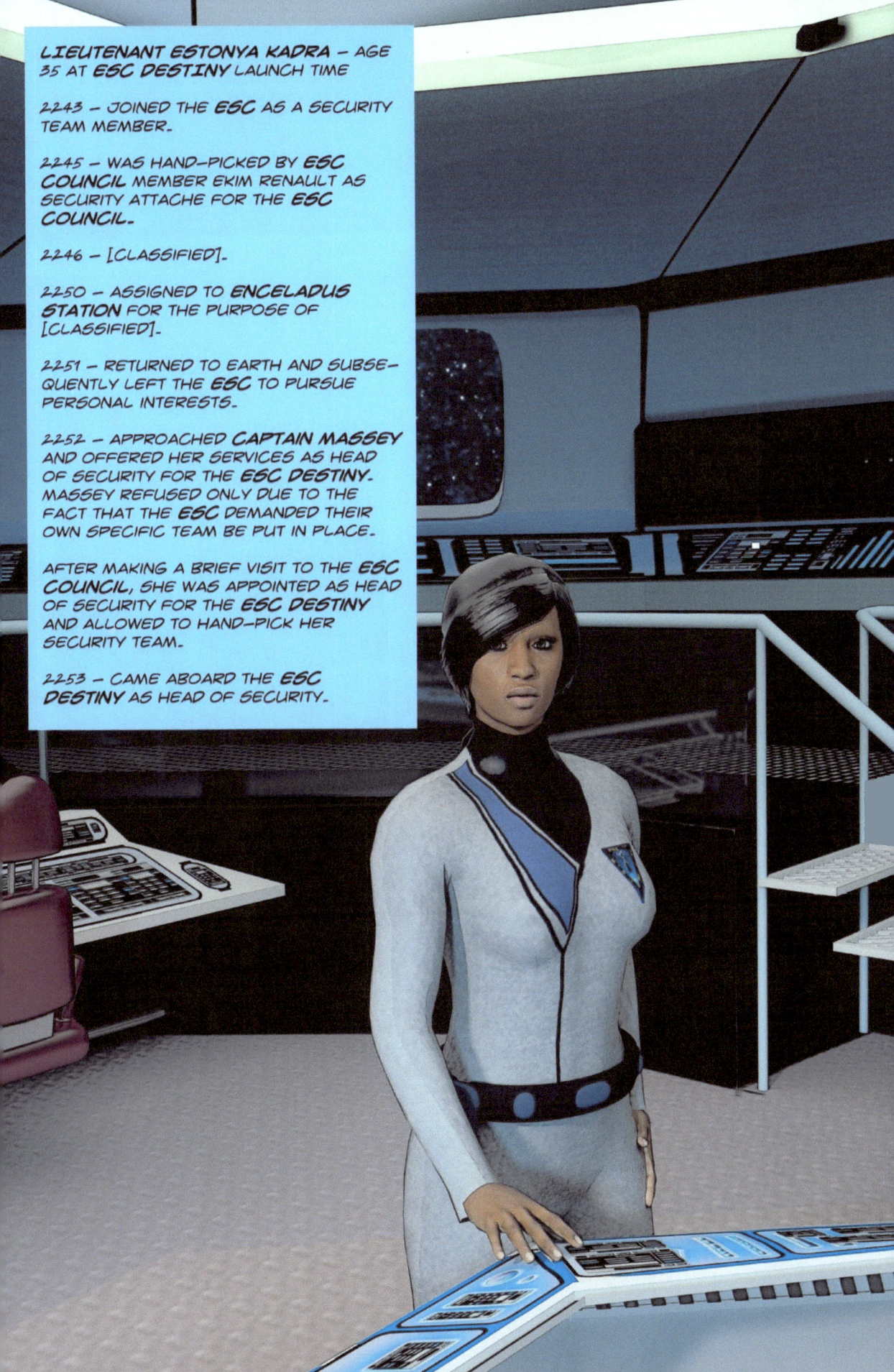

LIEUTENANT ESTONYA KADRA — AGE 35 AT *ESC DESTINY* LAUNCH TIME

2243 — JOINED THE *ESC* AS A SECURITY TEAM MEMBER.

2245 — WAS HAND-PICKED BY *ESC COUNCIL* MEMBER EKIM RENAULT AS SECURITY ATTACHE FOR THE *ESC COUNCIL*.

2246 — [CLASSIFIED].

2250 — ASSIGNED TO *ENCELADUS STATION* FOR THE PURPOSE OF [CLASSIFIED].

2251 — RETURNED TO EARTH AND SUBSE-QUENTLY LEFT THE *ESC* TO PURSUE PERSONAL INTERESTS.

2252 — APPROACHED *CAPTAIN MASSEY* AND OFFERED HER SERVICES AS HEAD OF SECURITY FOR THE *ESC DESTINY*. MASSEY REFUSED ONLY DUE TO THE FACT THAT THE *ESC* DEMANDED THEIR OWN SPECIFIC TEAM BE PUT IN PLACE.

AFTER MAKING A BRIEF VISIT TO THE *ESC COUNCIL*, SHE WAS APPOINTED AS HEAD OF SECURITY FOR THE *ESC DESTINY* AND ALLOWED TO HAND-PICK HER SECURITY TEAM.

2253 — CAME ABOARD THE *ESC DESTINY* AS HEAD OF SECURITY.

INTERVIEWS? WHAT YOU REALLY MEAN IS INTERROGATIONS!

CALL IT WHAT YOU WANT, CAPTAIN. I CAN GUARANTEE YOU, I WILL BE MAKING SOME CHANGES ON THIS SHIP!

THE HELL YOU WILL! LT. KADRA, PLEASE ADVISE THE PALOMINO WE WILL BE RETURNING OUR VISITORS AND WE WILL BE TAKING OUR CREWMEMBER BACK!

BEEP!

BRIDGE

IM SORRY, SIR. THE PALOMINO DISEMBARKED IMMEDIATELY ATER THE DELEGATES CAME ABOARD. THEY APPEAR TO HAVE SET A COURSE FOR EARTH.

IT SEEMS YOU ARE STUCK WITH ME, CAPTAIN.

IF YOU THINK I WON'T CHASE THAT SHIP DOWN AND —

CAPTAIN, WE'RE TRACKING TWO INCOMING VESSELS! ONE APPEARS TO BE AN ALLIANCE SHIP!
ON THE BRIDGE...
SIR, THE ALLIANCE VESSEL IS ATTACKING THE OTHER SHIP, WHICH APPEARS TO BE A SMALL TRANSPORT SHUTTLE!
MISTER PERRY, GET US IN FRONT OF THEIR COURSE. LT. KADRA, CONTACT THAT SHUTTLE AND LET THEM KNOW WE'RE GOING TO ASSIST.

LT. KADRA, FIRE ON THE ALLIANCE SHIP! TRY TO DISABLE HER WEAPONS! OPS, PREPARE TO GRAPPLE THAT SHUTTLE!
CAPTAIN! YOU CAN **NOT** FIRE ON THAT SHIP! THEY HAVEN'T TAKEN ANY AGGRESSIVE ACTION TOWARDS-

KA-THUNK!

KA-THUNK!

KA-THUNK!

CAPTAIN, THE SHUTTLE IS GRAPPLED. PULLING HER IN NOW.

CAPTAIN, I *DEMAND* YOU RELEASE MY SHIP NOW! YOU HAVE **NO RIGHT** TO INTERFERE WITH MY VESSEL!

YOU MAY WANT TO BE CAREFUL WHO YOU ARE TRYING TO THREATEN. I CAN HAVE YOU PUT AWAY SOMEWHERE YOU WILL *NEVER* SEE YOUR SHIP AGAIN, LET ALONE DAYLIGHT. I'VE LOOKED UP YOUR RECORD. YOU'RE A KNOWN DRUG-RUNNER! NO DOUBT WE'LL FIND A LOAD OF *STIMS* ABOARD YOUR SHIP!

I BROUGHT US INTO THE *TAE LOR* MINING SYSTEM. I FIGURED IT WAS THE BEST OPTION TO QUICKLY GET AWAY FROM THE ALLIANCE SHIP AND BRING US TO A PLACE WHERE WE COULD GET SOME REPAIRS DONE, BUT...

WHAT'S THE PROBLEM?

B—BECAUSE OF THE DAMAGE TO OUR THRUSTERS, I BROUGHT US IN HARD TO ACHIEVE AN ORBIT AROUND THE MINING COLONY...BUT I MISCALCULATED. WE'RE GOING INTO *ORBITAL DECAY*. I CAN'T ACHIEVE A STABLE ORBIT WITH ONLY ONE THRUSTER —

— AND WE CAN'T USE THE HYPER-G'S THIS CLOSE TO THE PLANET.

CORRECT, CAPTAIN. OUR GRAVITATIONAL ENVELOPE WOULD BE DEVASTATING TO THE PLANET'S ATMOSPHERE AT THIS RANGE.

TAE LOR HAS A MOON. MISTER PERRY, CAN YOU USE THE THRUSTER TO GET US INTO ONE OF THE LAGRANGE POINTS?

NO, I'M SORRY, CAPTAIN. IT'S IMPOSSIBLE TO BREAK—AWAY FROM THE GRAVITATIONAL PULL OF THE PLANET WITH ONLY *ONE* THRUSTER!

I CAN DO IT.

RIGHT. I'M SURE IT'S EASY FOR A SHUTTLE PILOT.

IT'S NOT EASY. IT'S EXTREMELY DIFFICULT, BUT IT'S NOT IMPOSSIBLE. I CAN DO IT.

ARE YOU SERIOUS?

I'M ALWAYS SERIOUS WHEN IT COMES TO PILOTING A SHIP, CAPTAIN.

CAPTAIN, YOU CAN'T POSSIBLY BE CONSIDERING GIVING HER NAVIGATIONAL CONTROL... THE DESTINY IS *NOT* A TRANSPORT SHUTTLE!

I'M WELL AWARE OF WHAT MY SHIP IS! STEP ASIDE, MISTER PERRY. MISS NORTH, YOU BETTER KNOW WHAT YOU'RE DOING.

CAPTAIN, I AGREE WITH MISTER PERRY'S ASSESSMENT. IF YOU LET THIS *DRUG RUNNER* TAKE CONTROL OF THIS SHIP, I'LL PUT YOU ON REPORT!

THEN REPORT ME! IN THE MEANTIME, BACK OFF AND LET ME DO MY JOB!

I'M GOING TO PUT US INTO A *HALO ORBIT* BY EXHAUSTING A FULL BURN ON THE PORT MID-THRUSTER TO ESCAPE THE PLANET'S GRAVITATIONAL PULL, LEAVING JUST ENOUGH TO STABILIZE US INTO ONE OF THE *LAGRANGE POINTS!* I'M GOING TO NEED ORBITAL EQUATIONS FED TO THIS PANEL! I HOPE YOU HAVE A GOOD *ASTROPHYSICIST* ONBOARD!

LT. ESTELLE?

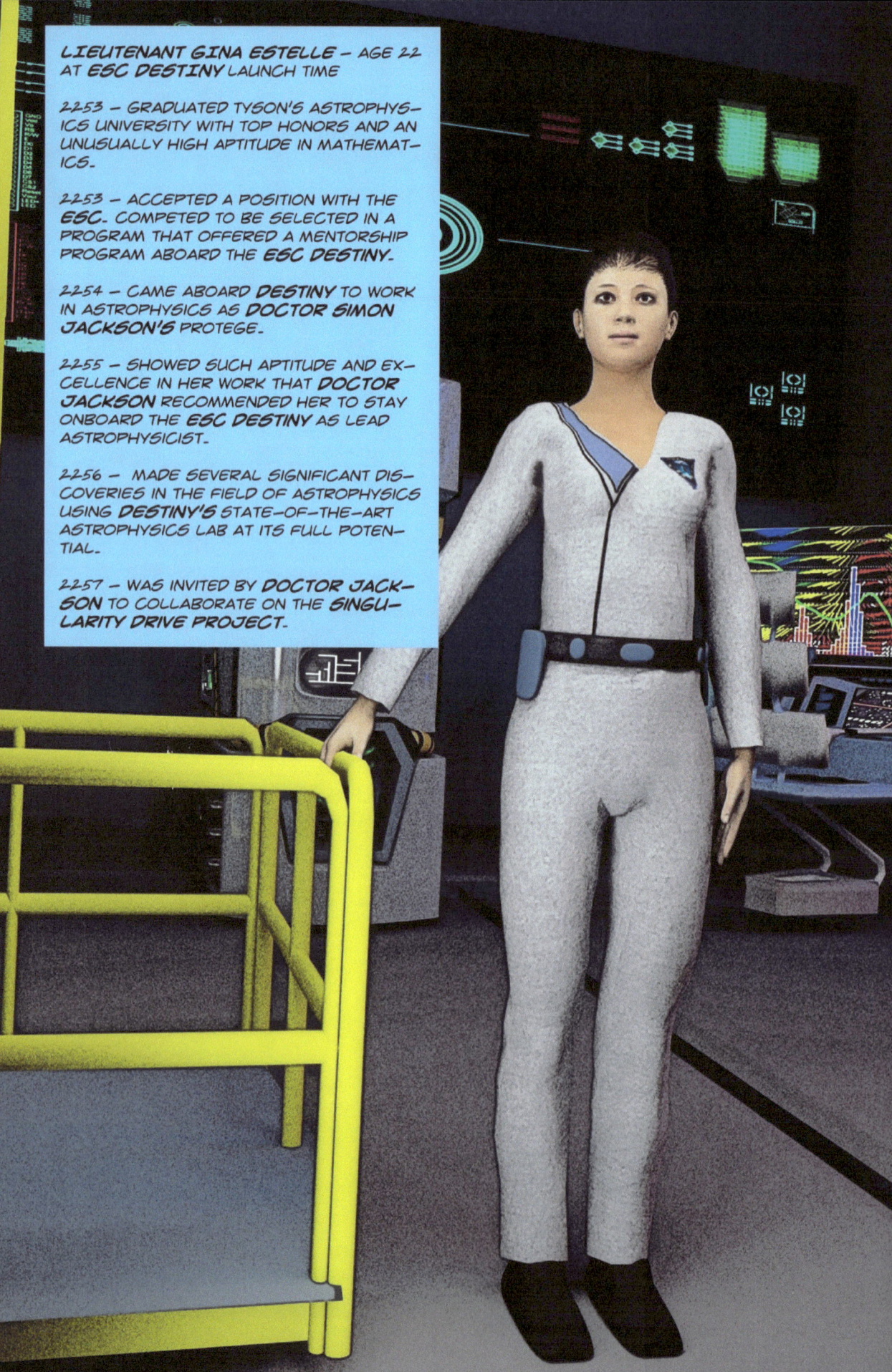

LIEUTENANT GINA ESTELLE – AGE 22 AT *ESC DESTINY* LAUNCH TIME

2253 – GRADUATED TYSON'S ASTROPHYSICS UNIVERSITY WITH TOP HONORS AND AN UNUSUALLY HIGH APTITUDE IN MATHEMATICS.

2253 – ACCEPTED A POSITION WITH THE *ESC*. COMPETED TO BE SELECTED IN A PROGRAM THAT OFFERED A MENTORSHIP PROGRAM ABOARD THE *ESC DESTINY*.

2254 – CAME ABOARD *DESTINY* TO WORK IN ASTROPHYSICS AS *DOCTOR SIMON JACKSON'S* PROTEGE.

2255 – SHOWED SUCH APTITUDE AND EXCELLENCE IN HER WORK THAT *DOCTOR JACKSON* RECOMMENDED HER TO STAY ONBOARD THE *ESC DESTINY* AS LEAD ASTROPHYSICIST.

2256 – MADE SEVERAL SIGNIFICANT DISCOVERIES IN THE FIELD OF ASTROPHYSICS USING *DESTINY'S* STATE-OF-THE-ART ASTROPHYSICS LAB AT ITS FULL POTENTIAL.

2257 – WAS INVITED BY *DOCTOR JACKSON* TO COLLABORATE ON THE *SINGULARITY DRIVE PROJECT*.

WORKING ON IT NOW, CAPTAIN. STANDBY...

CAPTAIN, I AM ISSUING YOU AN *EXECUTIVE ESC ORDER!* I WANT THAT WOMAN RE-MOVED FROM THE BRIDGE!

I NEED TO CONCENTRATE HERE OR THIS IS GOING TO END VERY BAD...

MISS ARROWAY, I NEED YOU TO LEAVE THE BRIDGE. NOW.

I AM A LEVEL III EMPLOYEE OF THE *ESC!* YOU *CANNOT* ORDER ME OFF THIS BRIDGE!

LT. KADRA, WOULD YOU PLEASE ESCORT MISS ARROWAY OFF THE BRIDGE?

SHE WILL DO NO SUCH THING!

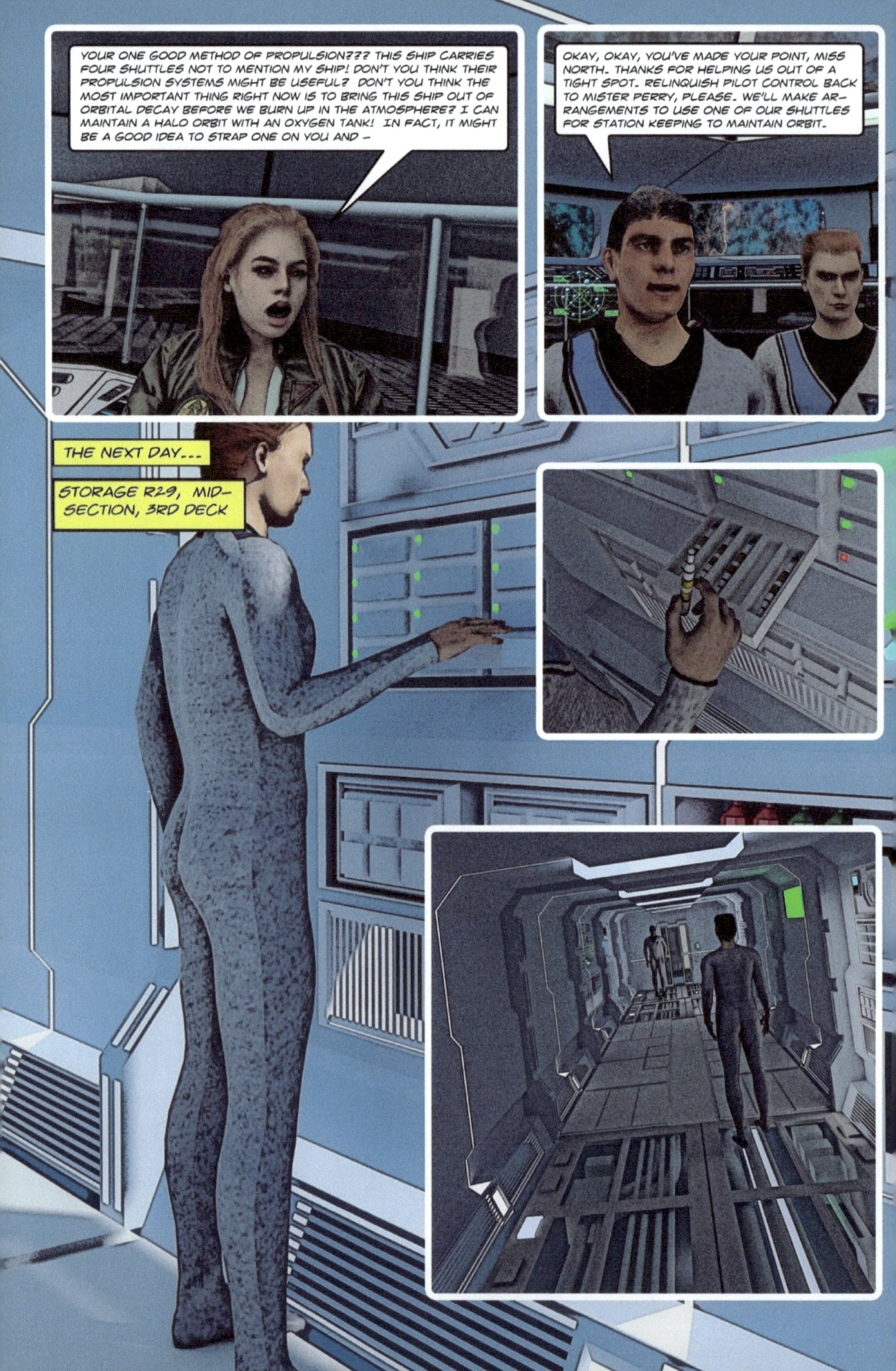

DOCTOR BENJAMIN DETRICK – AGE 52 AT **ESC DESTINY** LAUNCH TIME

2218 – VOLUNTEERED FOR THE RAINFOREST REVITALIZATION PROJECT IN BRAZIL

2223 – GRADUATED NEW HARVARD UNIVERSITY WITH A DEGREE IN MEDICINE.

2226 – BECAME DISENCHANTED WITH CORPORATE MEDICAL ENTITY WORK AND STARTED AN UNDERGROUND PRIVATE MEDICAL PRACTICE. DURING THESE YEARS, HE MOVED HIS PRACTICE TO SEVERAL AREAS HE FELT WERE BEING OVERLOOKED BY CORPORATE MEDICAL. THIS ALSO HAD THE ADVANTAGE OF KEEPING HIM ONE STEP AHEAD OF THE AUTHORITIES.

2232 – SUCCESSFULLY LED A CAMPAIGN FOR LEGISLATION CHANGE TO ALLOW FOR THE REINTRODUCTION OF PRIVATE MEDICAL PRACTICE ACROSS THE GLOBE. THIS ALSO LEGITIMIZED HIS OWN GROWING NETWORK OF PRIVATE PRACTICE WHICH BECAME A MODEL FOR OTHER GROWING PRIVATE MEDICAL FACILITIES.

2237 – WAS RECRUITED BY A GROWING FACTION KNOWN AS **"THE ALLIANCE"** TO PROVIDE MEDICAL SUPPORT. ALTHOUGH HE FELT THE CAUSE WAS A JUST ONE – RESISTANCE AGAINST THE **ESC** CONGLOMERATE THAT DOMINATED ALMOST EVERY FACET OF SCIENTIFIC ADVANCEMENT – HE FOUND HE COULD NOT CONDONE THEIR VIOLENT MEANS.

2240 – SEVERED TIES WITH POLITICAL CAUSES AND FOCUSED HIS ATTENTION ON SPECIALIZED AREAS.

2241 – AFTER DISCOVERING A GLARING ERROR IN THE CLASSIFICATION OF ALIEN MICROBES, CREATED PROJECT XENOMORPH TO PERFORM MORE IN-DEPTH XENOBIOLOGICAL STUDIES.

2252 – WAS APPROACHED BY **CAPTAIN MASSEY** TO LEAD THE DEPARTMENT OF XENOBIOLOGY FOR THE **ESC DESTINY** AS A NON-**ESC** CREWMEMBER.

2254 – WHEN AN ACCIDENT ABOARD THE **ESC DESTINY** TAKES THE LIFE OF LEAD PHYSICIAN **PAUL GARRANT**, **DOCTOR DETRICK** IS APPOINTED AS TEMPORARY HEAD OF MEDLAB. **CAPTAIN MASSEY** SUBSEQUENTLY REFUSED EACH NEW CANDIDATE SENT BY THE **ESC**.

ARROWAY'S OFFICE

HERE'S THE PROPOSED INTERVIEW SCHEDULE I'VE BEEN WORKING ON. IT STARTS WITH THE PRIMARY CREW-MEMBERS, AS YOU REQUESTED.

GOOD. CAMERON, I WANT YOU TO INSPECT THE SHIP. DO IT QUIETLY... GET A FEEL FOR THE WORKING CONDITIONS AND COMPETENCY OF THE CREW. BUT FIRST...

MA'AM?

FIND ME SOMETHING ON THIS SHIP THAT TASTES LIKE REAL COFFEE.

ASTROPHYSICS

...IF I'M RIGHT, IT WILL BE THE FIRST TIME A BINARY STAR SYSTEM'S ORBITAL PATH CAN BE ACCURATELY CALCULATED!

CONGRATULATIONS, LIEUTENANT. IF YOU KEEP THIS UP, THEY WILL START NAMING THINGS AFTER YOU.

I'VE MADE A BIT OF A BREAKTHROUGH MYSELF.

REALLY? TELL ME ABOUT IT.

OF COURSE, YOU KNOW ABOUT THE PERSISTENT GRAVITY WAVE THEORY SCIENTISTS RECENTLY DISCOVERED BACK ON EARTH?

ONLY ONE OF THE GREATEST DISCOVERIES OF OUR TIME!

WELL, YES. I'VE BEEN EXTRAPOLATING THE WAVE COEFFICIENT. I BELIEVE I'VE DETERMINED A WAY TO APPLY IT TO THE HYPER-GRAVITATIONAL PROPULSION SYSTEM. THIS WOULD HYPOTHETICALLY—

COMMANDER JACKSON! YOU CALL THIS A 'BIT OF A BREAK-THROUGH'??? THAT WOULD REVOLUTIONIZE SPACE TRAVEL!

WELL, AS I SAID, IT'S STILL IN THE HYPOTHETICAL STAGE. IT WOULD ALSO HAVE HYPER-INERTIAL ENERGY APPLICATIONS EVERYWHERE. ENERGY CONSUMPTION WOULD NO LONGER BE A PROBLEM.

THIS IS AMAZING NEWS! WHAT DOES THE CAPTAIN THINK? HAVE YOU PUT TOGETHER A TEAM TO WORK ON THIS?

I HAVEN'T TOLD THE CAPTAIN YET. I HAVEN'T TOLD ANYONE... UNTIL NOW.

I'M THE FIRST PERSON YOU TOLD ABOUT THIS?

I WANTED TO TELL YOU FIRST BECAUSE... I WANT TO ASK YOU SOMETHING. I KNOW YOUR WORK IN ASTROPHYSICS KEEPS YOU QUITE BUSY, BUT I'VE NOTICED YOU ALSO HAVE AN APTITUDE FOR UNDERSTANDING HYPER DIMENSIONAL EQUATIONS...

WELL, I'VE ALWAYS BEEN INTERESTED IN LEARNING MORE ON THAT SIDE OF THINGS, BUT—

DON'T SELL YOURSELF SHORT, LIEUTENANT. THERE ARE NOT MANY WHO CAN GRASP THE CONCEPTS OR DO THE MATH —AND YOU CAN DO BOTH. I NEED SOME ONE ON MY TEAM WHO CAN DO THAT...AND I DON'T WANT TO DO THIS ALONE. I WOULD LIKE YOU TO COLLABORATE WITH ME ON THIS.

COLLABORATE WITH YOU? I DON'T KNOW WHAT TO SAY...

I'M HOPING YOU'LL SAY YES...

YES! OF COURSE! I WOULD BE HONORED!

GOOD. I'LL PLAN A MEETING WITH THE CAPTAIN AND MAKE A REQUEST FOR YOU TO BE ON THE TEAM.

COMMANDER JACKSON...

YES, LIEUTENANT?

THANK YOU SO MUCH FOR THIS. I MEAN THAT. IT'S BE- CAUSE OF YOU THAT I'M ON THIS SHIP. YOU ARE TRULY ONE OF THE GENIUSES OF OUR TIME.

GENIUS? THANK YOU FOR THE COMPLI- MENT LIEUTENANT, BUT I DON'T FEEL LIKE ONE. IN FACT, I FEEL QUITE THE OPPOSITE THESE DAYS...

YOU WANT ME TO **WHAT???**

I NEED A REAL PILOT ON THIS SHIP. WHAT YOU DID OUT THERE — NOT JUST WITH THE **DESTINY**, BUT DURING YOUR RUN—IN WITH THAT ALLIANCE SHIP — I'VE NEVER SEEN ANYTHING LIKE IT AND I'VE DONE A FEW WILD MANEUVERS IN MY TIME.

I'D RATHER **DIE** THAN SPEND ONE MORE MINUTE ON THIS SHIP! WHAT MAKES YOU THINK I WOULD EVER WORK FOR THE CONSORTIUM???

MISS NORTH... WHAT DO YOU KNOW ABOUT THIS SHIP?

I KNOW EVERYTHING ABOUT IT. HYPER—GRAVITATIONAL PROPULSION, DEEP SPACE CAPABILITY, CREW COMPLEMENT—

I'M NOT TALKING ABOUT TECH SPECS. I MEAN, WHAT DO YOU KNOW ABOUT OUR PURPOSE?

JUST LIKE ANY OTHER *CONSORTIUM* SHIP....OUT HERE STEALING RESOURCES FOR THE CORPORATE *ESC PIGS* BACK ON EARTH!

COMMANDER JACKSON AND MYSELF CONVINCED THE *ESC* TO COMMISSION THE *DESTINY.* WE BOTH HAD OUR OWN REASONS....HE NEEDED A LARGE PRODUCTION VESSEL TO IMPLEMENT HIS HYPER-G TECHNOLOGY AND I WANTED TO COMMAND A SHIP OF EXPLORATION.

EXPLORATION??? YOU'RE TELLING ME THE *ESC* JUST LETS YOU FLY THIS SHIP AROUND FOR SCIENCE? THAT'S A LOAD OF BULL—

—YES, WE HAVE TO DISCOVER POSSIBLE RESOURCE AVENUES FOR THE *ESC* AND PROTECT ITS MINING OPERATIONS, BUT THAT'S NOT ALL WE DO OUT HERE! WE'RE PUSHING THE BOUNDRIES OF SPACE. AND THE *ESC* COUNCIL WITH ALL THEIR DIRECTIVES AND EXECUTIVES SIT A LONG WAY AWAY FROM HERE. DO YOU UNDERSTAND WHAT I'M SAYING?

IT SEEMS TO ME ONE OF THEIR TOP EXECUTIVES SITS RIGHT ACROSS THE CORRIDOR. AND IF SHE HAS HER WAY, I'M GOING AWAY FOR A REALLY LONG TIME, CAPTAIN.

YES, THAT DOES SEEM TO BE WHERE YOU'RE HEADED AFTER WHAT WE FOUND ABOARD YOUR SHIP. YOU MAY WANT TO GIVE MY OFFER A LITTLE MORE THOUGHT.

MISTER RICHARD ANTWERP CAMERON III –
AGE 32 AT ESC DESTINY LAUNCH TIME

2239 – JOINED *ESC* AS AN ADMINISTRATIVE CLERK

2254 – MISTAKEN AS AN EXECUTIVE ASSISTANT, WAS ORDERED BY **MISS ARROWAY** TO GET HER COFFEE, WHICH HE DID. SHE WAS SURPRISED THAT HE ACTU-ALLY MADE THE COFFEE CORRECTLY TO HER SPECIFI-CATIONS AND SUBSEQUENTLY TOOK HIM FROM HIS PO-SITION IN ADMINISTRATION TO BECOME HER PERSONAL ASSISTANT.

2256 – CAME ABOARD THE *ESC DESTINY* WITH **MISS ARROWAY** FOR THE PURPOSE OF INVESTIGATING THE SHIP AND CREW TO ENSURE *ESC* INTERESTS WERE BEING LOOKED AFTER.

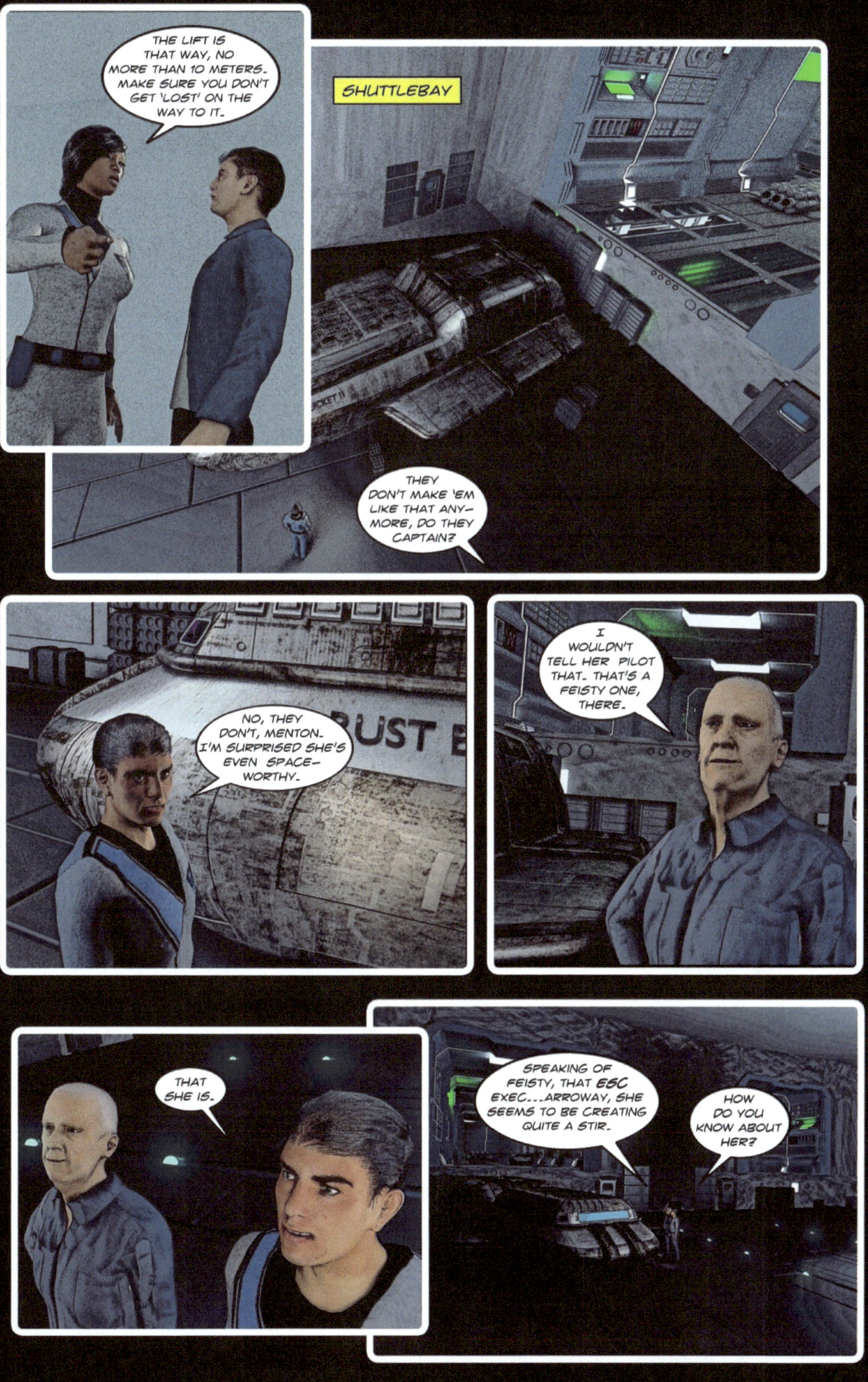

THE LIFT IS THAT WAY, NO MORE THAN 10 METERS. MAKE SURE YOU DON'T GET 'LOST' ON THE WAY TO IT.

THEY DON'T MAKE 'EM LIKE THAT ANYMORE, DO THEY CAPTAIN?

NO, THEY DON'T, MENTON. I'M SURPRISED SHE'S EVEN SPACEWORTHY.

I WOULDN'T TELL HER PILOT THAT. THAT'S A FEISTY ONE, THERE.

THAT SHE IS.

SPEAKING OF FEISTY, THAT ESC EXEC...ARROWAY, SHE SEEMS TO BE CREATING QUITE A STIR.

HOW DO YOU KNOW ABOUT HER?

WHOLE SHIP IS TALKING ABOUT HER — HOW THE FIRST THING SHE DID WAS FIRE THE GUY THAT WELCOMED HER ONBOARD. I HEAR YOU'VE HAD SOME RUN-INS WITH HER TOO.

NOTHING I CAN'T HANDLE. SHE'S JUST HERE BE-CAUSE THE **ESC** THINKS WE'RE PLAYING GAMES OUT HERE.

WELL, I HOPE FOR YOUR SAKE SHE DOESN'T PRY TOO DEEP INTO THINGS. SHE MIGHT NOT LIKE WHAT SHE FINDS...

OBSERVATION DECK

NICE VIEW, ISN'T IT?

I'VE SEEN BETTER.

MAYBE SO, BUT I'M SURE THIS VIEW IS *MUCH* BETTER THAN THE VIEW FROM INSIDE A CELL. I UNDERSTAND THE CAPTAIN WANTS YOU TO STAY ON AS PILOT.

YEAH, WELL EVEN IF I WANTED TO DO THAT — WHICH I DON'T — THERE'S A BIG PROBLEM WITH THAT IDEA. I MIGHT BE ABLE TO WORK TO PAY-OFF REGISTRATION FINES AND WHAT-EVER OTHER FALSE CHARGES THE *ESC* HAS AGAINST ME, BUT THE *STIMS* THEY CLAIM I WAS SMUGGLING MEANS SERIOUS CON-FINEMENT.

IT'S POSSIBLE THE PURPORTED *STIMS* GOT MISPLACED, MAYBE JETTISONED OUT OF AN AIRLOCK. MAYBE THEY NEVER EVEN EXISTED. THAT IS, IF YOU MAKE THE RIGHT CHOICE...

ARE YOU TRYING TO *BLACKMAIL* ME, COMMANDER JACKSON?!

QUITE THE OPPOSITE. IF ANYTHING, I'M EXPANDING YOUR AVENUES OF OPPORTUNITY. AND YOU KNOW WHAT THEY SAY ABOUT OPPORTUNITY, MISS NORTH —IT DOESN'T KNOCK TWICE.

CAPTAIN, HAVE YOU BEEN AVOIDING ME? I'VE PUT IN A NUMBER OF REQUESTS FOR YOU TO COME TO MY OFFICE OVER THE PAST FEW DAYS.

SIGH WHAT CAN I DO FOR YOU, MISS ARROWAY?

I NEED TO SCHEDULE SOME TIME WITH YOU FOR YOUR INTERVIEW!

OH, THE INTERROGATION? I GUESS IT MUST HAVE SLIPPED MY MIND. WHY DON'T YOU START WITH JAX? MY SCHEDULE IS PRETTY FULL.

YOU CAN TRY TO AVOID THIS ALL YOU WANT, CAPTAIN, BUT I AM NOT GOING AWAY!

I SHOULD BE SO LUCKY!

SO...HAVE YOU GIVEN MY OFFER SOME THOUGHT, MISS NORTH?

IT SEEMS I DON'T HAVE MUCH OF A CHOICE CAPTAIN. I'M A PILOT....AND I CAN'T DO THAT FROM LOCK-UP.

IS THAT A YES?

I'M ONLY GOING TO DO THIS AS LONG AS IT TAKES TO BUY MY FREEDOM BACK AND TO GET MY SHIP SPACE-WORTHY AGAIN. AFTER THAT, I'M GONE.

FAIR ENOUGH, I GUESS.

AND... I HAVE ONE DEMAND.

DEMAND?? DO YOU REALLY THINK YOU'RE IN A POSITION TO....OH NEVERMIND, WHAT IS IT?

I'M NOT WEARING THAT DAMNED UNIFORM.

COMMANDER, I WAS JUST RE-VIEWING THE SECURE INVENTORIES...

YES?

IT APPEARS THE ENTIRE SHIPMENT OF *STIMS* THE PILOT WAS SMUGGLING HAS DISAPPEARED. YOUR KEYCODE WAS THE LAST ONE USED TO ACCESS THAT LOCATION.

YES, I'VE MOVED THE SHIPMENT TO ANOTHER SECURE LOCATION PENDING THE OUTCOME OF THE PILOT'S CASE. YOU CAN...TALK TO THE CAPTAIN ABOUT IT IF YOU WANT TO CONFIRM.

THAT WON'T BE NECESSARY, SIR. BUT AS CHIEF OF SECURITY, I WOULD APPRECIATE BEING KEPT IN THE LOOP ABOUT SOMETHING LIKE THIS.

YOU'RE QUITE RIGHT, LIEUTENANT. THAT WAS AN OVERSIGHT ON MY PART —BUT PLAUSIBLE DENIABILITY MIGHT BE A GOOD THING IN THIS CASE. THIS WHOLE 'NON-*ESC* PILOT' THING THE CAPTAIN HAS DONE ISN'T EXACTLY ER... PROCEDURE.

I KNOW YOU DON'T WANT TO BE HERE, BUT... WELL, I'M GLAD YOU ARE. WELCOME ABOARD.

ONCE OUT OF THE TAE LOR SYSTEM, THE *DESTINY'S* HYPER—GRAVITATIONAL PROPULSION SYSTEM IS BROUGHT ONLINE AND THE SHIP SURGES INTO THE OUTER REACHES OF SPACE.

TO BE CONTINUED...

NEXT EPISODE...

"NOW, *DOCTOR JACKSON*...LET'S BEGIN AGAIN. I WANT YOU TO TELL ME EVERY-THING YOU KNOW ABOUT DESTINY'S HYPER GRAPVITATIONAL PROPULSION SYSTEMS."

DR. PETRICK   CMDR. ZHANG   LT. ESTELLE   CMDR. JACKSON   CAPT. MASSEY   MISS ARROWAY   MISTER CAMERON   LT. KADRA   MISS NORTH

A MESSAGE FROM THE CREATORS...

DESTINY WAS TRULY BORN IN 1981...
I CAN REMEMBER QUITE CLEARLY SITTING IN MY BEDROOM AS A TEENAGER.
THE MUSIC OF COSMOS, THE SOUNDTRACK TO CARL SAGEN'S **COSMOS**
SERIES, PLAYED FROM MY RECORD PLAYER AS I LEANED BACK WITH HEAD-
PHONES ON. AS THE SOFT SYNTH MUSIC OF THE TRACK CALLED **LEGACY**
FILLED MY EARS, A SCENE BEGAN TO FORM IN MY MIND.
I SAW A SHIP, DARK AND DESOLATE, FLIPPING END OVER END IN DEEP SPACE.
AND I THOUGHT, **WHY** IS THIS SHIP HERE? **WHAT** HAPPENED TO CAUSE THIS
SHIP TO BE DEAD? WHAT HAPPENED TO HER? **WHERE** IS HER CREW? AND
DOES ANYONE KNOW...DOES ANYONE **CARE**?
FROM THAT BRIEF BIT OF INSPIRATION, EVERYTHING THAT **DESTINY** IS OR
EVER WILL BE, STARTED. IT AMAZES ME STILL...
SO, IN A STRANGE KIND OF WAY, CARL SAGEN HELPED TO CREATE **DESTINY**.
SO DID GENE RODDENBERRY. AND ROD SERLING....AND A HOST OF OTHER
PEOPLE THAT HAVE HELPED TO IGNITE THE SPARK OF MY OWN IMAGINATION IN
DIFFERENT WAYS.
I NEVER WANT TO LOSE THEIR INSPIRATION...

MICHAEL GLOVER

Michael Glover

THE **SECRETS** OF **DESTINY**...

I'VE ALWAYS LIKED THE IDEA OF FINDING EASTER EGGS — THOSE LITTLE
HIDDEN TRINKETS BURIED WITHIN BOOKS, FILM AND OTHER MEDIUMS. THINGS
LIKE THE **R2D2** ROBOT OF **STAR WARS** SITTING INCONSPICUOUSLY ON THE
MOTHERSHIP IN THE MOVIE, **CLOSE ENCOUNTERS OF THE THIRD KIND**.
SO, IT'S NO SURPRISE **DESTINY** HAS SECRETS ALSO. SOME MAY BE OBVI-
OUS, SOME MAY NEVER BE FOUND. STILL OTHERS MIGHT BE INSIDE JOKES
THAT WOULDN'T MAKE SENSE TO THE AVERAGE READER EVEN IF THEY WERE
FOUND. THE CHARACTERS HAVE SECRETS, TOO. OH YES, THEY HAVE SE-
CRETS. AS THE STORY UNFOLDS, WE'LL LEARN MORE ABOUT THEM. SOME
MAY DELIGHT US, SOME MAY INTRIGUE, BUT SOME WE MAY WISH WE NEVER
FOUND OUT. I'M HAPPY TO SAY THAT WHEN I WRITE A SCRIPT FOR DESTINY,
I'M JUST AS SURPRISED TO FIND OUT THESE THINGS AS YOU MIGHT BE.
THESE CHARACTERS KNOW WHO THEY ARE, WHAT THEY'VE DONE AND WHERE
THEY ARE GOING. THEY ONLY USE US TO GET THEIR STORY TOLD AND THAT
IS AS IT SHOULD BE. I CAN'T WAIT TO FIND OUT WHAT HAPPENS NEXT....

D.V. NOBLES

D V Nob

www.ingramcontent.com/pod-product-compliance
Lightning Source LLC
Chambersburg PA
CBHW040959170626
46815CB00002B/82